Mrs. Ashbury's World

Connect with the World of Mrs. Ashbury in one of the ways below:

WWW.MRSASHBURYSWORLD.COM 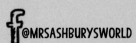@MRSASHBURYSWORLD 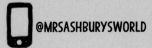@MRSASHBURYSWORLD 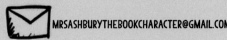MRSASHBURYTHEBOOKCHARACTER@GMAIL.COM

Mrs. Ashbury's First Day of School

Written by: Rekia Beverly

Illustrated by: Shalon Wright

Printed in the United States of America
ISBN-13: 9781728830391

Mrs. Ashbury couldn't wait to meet her new class of students. After all, she had been planning to meet them since the last day of school the previous year.

Endless nights she researched different ways to greet her students. "Good morning boys and girls," in a giddy voice. Or a prestigious "Good morning scholars!"

Either way, everything needed to be perfect.

During the summer months, Mrs. Ashbury traveled to many places. She went to Arizona to see the Grand Canyon and experienced her first train ride.

Even though
Mrs. Ashbury enjoyed all
of those things, she was still
anxious about the
first day of school.

"Should my walls be full of color? Should I use a beach theme? Oh wait, maybe an owl theme," she thought.
Mrs. Ashbury felt the pressure . . . time was ticking, the months were flying by and soon it would be the first day of school!

"Mom! Dad! I need a lunch box, a new backpack and those cool new pencils I just saw on TV and . . . new sneakers too. I need all of it for the first day of school!" said Keith.

"Honey, we have at least a month before school starts."
His parents tried everything to calm him down. They went
bowling, to the park, and to the movie theatre.
None of those activities could keep Keith's enthusiasm down,
so they decided to take him to music camp.

Even when Keith went to music camp, he still kept talking about his first day of school.
The camp advisors came up with a song to keep Keith calm.

Singing did not help either! The camp advisors decided to talk to Keith's parents when they picked him up from camp. "Your camper talked about the first day of school every second of everyday," they said. Keith just smiled.

On the way back from music camp, Keith only had one thing on his mind, and that was school! While riding, Keith began to daydream of all of the new things he was going to learn when school started. Keith's daydream was suddenly interrupted when he heard a BOOM! His parents yelled out, "FLAT TIRE." That was not the news Keith wanted to hear. In a panic, he started asking questions, "Will I be able to make it to the first day of school?"
"Will I be able to meet my new teacher?"

"Calm down," his parents insisted. They explained to him that a flat tire would only take a few minutes to change and they would be back on the road in no time. They assured Keith that he would be able to make it to the first day of school and meet his new teacher.

Days and days passed by.
Both Keith and
Mrs. Ashbury were
counting down.
Only 3 days left until the first day of school!

Just 3 days left! Mrs. Ashbury had her checklist of things:
bulletin board-Check, names on desks-check.
Keith had his checklist also: lunchbox-check, backpack-check.

Only 2 days left! Mrs. Ashbury had added more to her checklist: laminating cut out-check, reading center organized-check. Keith added more to his checklist also: uniform-check, sneakers-check.

Just 1 day left until school starts on Monday! Mrs. Ashbury's list only had two things left to check off: a new dress-check and her best smile-check, check, check!

Keith's list had one item to left to check off: go to bed early-CHECK!

Keith	Nathan
Rhonda	Danielle

The classroom was fully decorated with a nautical theme.
Every desk was labeled with student names.
The whiteboard had "Welcome to your First Day of School" in green writing with a beautiful picture of an anchor.

Ralphie	Rosemary
Donald	Kim

Janet	Rick
Ann	James

Reggie	Ashley
Nick	Donna

Mrs. Ashbury stood at the door and greeted all of her students,
even Keith.
They both froze.
Simultaneously they both said, "I've been waiting for this day!
I always get excited for the first day of school. I'm so glad to meet you!"

All the students paused and watched as Mrs. Ashbury and Keith said the same exact thing! By the time they stopped talking all the kids burst into a cheer, "It's going to be a great year!"

All of the students in Mrs. Ashbury's class enjoyed their first day of school, especially Keith. He shared his dreams and interests with his new classmates. He also drew a picture of his family.

His favorite part of the day was telling his friends about music camp and how he almost did not make it to the first day of school because of the flat tire.

When the bell rang and school dismissed,
Keith could not wait to get home.

While throwing his backpack on the sofa, he told his parents everything. He told them how his teacher felt just as anxious as he did for the first day of school to arrive.

"Mom! Dad, my teacher and I froze in time! "Slow down Keith!
You are talking too fast," said his mom. "Mom, it was so cool!
We said the same exact thing at the same exact time!"
His parents giggled.
"Wow, it sounds like you
enjoyed your first day of school!"
Keith shouted a big, "YES!"

After that conversation, Keith and his parents knew it was going to be a great year.

Mrs. Ashbury knew it would be a great year, too.

ABOUT THE AUTHOR

Mrs. Ashbury is the brainchild of career educator and writer, Rekia Beverly.
A native of New Smyrna Beach, Florida.
Mrs. Ashbury is dear to Beverly's heart because many of her shared experiences with students are modeled after her actual teaching encounters.
Beverly created Mrs. Ashbury's character as a tool to empower students and parents with a different perspective of how teachers actually view themselves.
Her goal is to give awareness to readers that teachers live normal lives too. They are excited, unsure, and learn lessons throughout the year just like their students.
Beverly is pleased to share Mrs. Ashbury with families and students. Her dream is to continue the adventures of Mrs. Ashbury's class for many years to come.

Connect with the World of Mrs. Ashbury in one of the ways below:

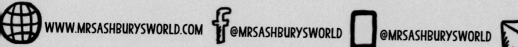 WWW.MRSASHBURYSWORLD.COM 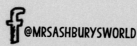@MRSASHBURYSWORLD 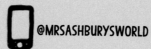@MRSASHBURYSWORLD MRSASHBURYTHEBOOKCHARACTER@GMAIL.COM

40177632R00020